CW01558998

This Book Belongs to

_____

# Dedication

I would like to dedicate this book to my teacher Mary Padlak, who taught me a new way of looking at the world and the wonderful possibilities of the human spirit and soul.

# A Note About This Book...

While this story has a very charming nature, this book can be additionally effective when used as a teaching tool, either by a parent, counselor, or psychologist. There are questions in the back of the book that can be used to promote further discussion. The concepts of shame, blame, and guilt are all addressed by the situations in the story, although never mentioned by name. Children by their very nature are narcissistic and thereby take responsibility, good or bad, for what happens in their world. As adults, we can assist them in learning boundaries and help them to perceive their world more accurately at the level they are ready to understand.

# Acknowledgments

There are many people to thank for their ongoing support of my efforts to publish this book. My weekly women's group, who listened to my reading the book, who offered sage advice, who contributed ideas, who helped with fine-tuning the illustrations, and who spent extra time with me to hammer out the small details that come with publication: Wendy Dombrowski, Cheryl Moss, Luisa Cleaves, Earlene Evans, Kellie Mahon, Mary Talavera, Terry Feiner, Jana Veale, and Sage DeFreitas (honorary member). I'm so grateful to my women's group of 30 years, whose insights and support have kept me afloat on this journey we call Life. Thank you Mary Padlak, Estelle Fineberg, Sherrill Kohler Valdes, and Barbara Windham. Thank you Tony Talavera for your skills with the written word and your steadiness of spirit. Lastly, I would like to thank my family for their ongoing support and love. Special thanks to my sister, Diane Nadler—I'm so grateful to have her in my life.

**www.mascotbooks.com**

*Angela the Warrior*

©2018 Stephanie Jordan. All Rights Reserved. No part of this publication may be reproduced, stored in a retrieval system or transmitted in any form by any means electronic, mechanical, or photocopying, recording or otherwise without the permission of the author.

**For more information, please contact:**

Mascot Books
620 Herndon Parkway, Suite 320
Herndon, VA 20170
info@mascotbooks.com

Library of Congress Control Number: 2017918179

CPSIA Code: PRT1217A
ISBN-13: 978-1-68401-752-2

Printed in the United States

# Angela the Warrior

Stephanie Jordan
PSYD, OMD

Illustrated by Qura-tul
Ain Shahnawaz

My name is Angela, and I'm a warrior. I'm ten years old, and this is my life story.

I used to worry about everything, and it would take up a lot of my time. I was afraid bad things might happen, and I would always have to be on the lookout for that next bad thing.

Then I found Annie. Annie used to talk to me about how to be brave and strong and how smart and pretty I was.

But I didn't believe her. After all, she was just a voice inside my head.

When I was four years old, my mother got very sick. She was in bed all the time, and she didn't play with me anymore.

I thought she didn't care about me. Sometimes I was hungry, but she couldn't get out of bed to get me something to eat.

Annie tried to tell me that Mom didn't have the energy to take care of me, but I didn't understand. I thought it was my fault. I thought there must be something wrong with me.

My parents divorced right before I turned seven years old, and
my mother and I moved far away from our old house.

I couldn't understand what happened, and I thought it was my fault. After all, we moved away the morning after I had a temper tantrum. I remember my mother throwing her hands up and saying she couldn't take it anymore.

Then I didn't have my dad in my life anymore. I felt like a terrible person. I felt that I wasn't good enough for him to want to be in my life. I felt unlovable.

Annie tried to tell me that I was just a kid and that my parents made these decisions because they were feeling bad. She told me they were just hurting because their marriage didn't work out and that they were not thinking about me. They were not paying any attention to what I was feeling. I could not imagine that.

when I was eight, I had to take tests at school that would decide if I was in the smart group of kids. My mother, who was a teacher, made me memorize a lot of questions and answers to some tests she had found. She must have thought I wasn't smart enough. I believed I wasn't good at anything I did. I thought she was ashamed and fearful that I wasn't smart enough... and so was I.

After a while, Annie—that voice inside my head—
noticed I was not happy anymore. Why was I sad so
much? Why was I spending so much time alone?

One day my mom told me that I would be meeting with the school counselor. You see, Mom was concerned about my grades since they were not very good anymore. She also noticed my sadness and that I didn't seem to enjoy doing the things I used to like doing.

I was very nervous before my meeting because I thought the counselor would be mad at me. Turns out she was NOT mad at me, and we played games and drew pictures together! Though it took me a while to want to talk to her, when I finally did, I started to feel a little bit better.

And you know what???? She repeated to me all the things Annie had been telling me my whole life!!!! I started to believe that my parents' divorce did not have anything to do with me. Mom and I did NOT move away because I was a bad girl. My parents had a lot of hurt feelings and they forgot that I had hurt feelings too.

But best of all, I learned that **Annie was ME and that I was Annie.**

I realized that I knew a lot of things about myself, but I hadn't learned to trust them yet because I was still a kid. Now that I'm ten, I listen more to the messages I get inside my head. My counselor has taught me to ask questions when I get confused, scared, or worried. When I do that, it does make me feel better. So, while sometimes I still don't understand everything, I no longer worry.

Instead of a worrier, I am now a Warrior! Yay me!!

# Questions and Ideas for Discussion

1. Do you think everyone you know has the same thoughts and ideas? People think differently. We don't know what someone else is thinking. It helps to ask.

2. Angela thought her mom didn't get out of her bed because she didn't care about her. What do you think her mom was thinking?

3. Do you worry like Angela? What do you worry about?

4. Do you think your friends worry? What do they worry about?

5. Do you ever think that what is happening is your fault?

6. Can you think of an example of something that was your fault? Can you think of a reason why it may not have been your fault?

7. How do you know what someone else is thinking? Instead of worrying about what they are thinking, you can ask questions. Asking is better than being scared or worrying.

8. What can you do when you are sad? What could you do differently when you are feeling this way? Talk about it with someone!

9. Have you ever talked to another person about your feelings? If so, was that a good experience for you?

10. Do you ask questions when you are confused, scared, or worried?

11. Who do you talk to about your feelings?

We all have a voice inside our heads that comments on different things we are doing. Instead of worrying about things, we can ask questions. We don't have to remain scared or confused. Asking questions is taking an action. By taking an action, you are no longer a worrier.

**You are a Warrior! Just like Angela!**

# About the Author

Dr. Stephanie Jordan has her Doctorate of Psychology and is also an Oriental Medicine Doctor. After a 20 year career as a clinical psychologist, she trained an additional four years to become proficient in Acupuncture and Chinese Herbs. Dr. Jordan has a unique presentation of everyday issues children confront that can have a huge impact. Sometimes the adults in their lives do not realize the degree to which children are affected. This is the first in a series of books planned to assist adults in dealing with challenging situations in the lives of children.